TABBY

A Story in Pictures by

ALIKI

HarperCollins*Publishers*

for Alexa Nicole Scott
and my two Emmas — Emma Jackson and Emma Powers

TABBY. Copyright © 1995 by Aliki Brandenberg. Printed in the U.S.A. All rights reserved. Library of Congress Cataloging-in-Publication Data   Aliki.
Tabby : a story in pictures / by Aliki.   p.   cm.   Summary: Pictures tell the story of a kitten's first year in her new home, with a warm bed, good
food, and a little girl to play with and love.   ISBN 0-06-024915-3. — ISBN 0-06-024916-1 (lib. bdg   [1. Cats—Fiction. 2. Stories without words.]
I. Title. PZ7.A397Tab 1995 [E]—dc20 94-18523 CIP AC Typography by Elynn Cohen I 2 3 4 5 6 7 8 9 10 ❖ First Edition